I0659143

Sedução
(Seduction)
An *Ain't Nobody* Prequel

Adrienne Thompson

Pink Cashmere Publishing, LLC
Arkansas, USA

Cover art by AA Thompson (**thompson9699@gmail.com**)

Printed in the United States of America

First Printing 2015

Copyright © 2015 Adrienne Thompson

ISBN: 0-9971461-8-4
ISBN-13: 978-0-9971461-8-9

has seen his fair share of torment looks to find the truth behind the deaths in his town. Devin knows she has to be one step ahead of the law as she seeks to solve the murders, but with Kaden hot on her tail, she begins to find it hard to stay away from the relentless detective who manages to make her heart race with every wicked touch he gives her. Her isolated life, duty to the pack and elicit vow of "no attachments" are about to be tested. And when Devin finds herself as the killer's next target, the showdown begins of who's Alpha and who's Omega.

Don't miss out!

You can sign up to receive emails whenever Kharma Kelley publishes a new book. There's no charge and no obligation.

Praise You, God, for keeping the stories coming! I will forever Praise You for the blessings You've given me.

For the fans of *Ain't Nobody*.
Thank you.

"A person may think their own ways are right, but the Lord weighs the heart."

Proverbs 21:2 NIV

Soundtrack:

"A Day in Rio" *Les Baxter*
"Rede de Espera" (Waiting Web) *Azymuth*
"Rio After Dark" *Lalo Schifrin*
"Incident in Rio" *Skeewiff*
"Knee Deep In Rio" *Maynard Ferguson*
"Brazilian Soul" *DJ Rhythm presents Brazilian Soul*
"Bom Conselho" (Good Advice) *Maria Bethânia*
"Real in Rio" *Sergio Mendes*
"Recado" (Message) *Jack Jezzro*
"Rendezvous In Rio" *Michael Franks*
"Río-Líze" *Vital Information*
"Depois do Carnaval" (After Carnival) Azymuth

1

"A Day in Rio"

2003, Rio de Janeiro, Brazil

The streets of Rio de Janeiro were buzzing with anticipation. Carnival would begin in a few days, and this meant dancing, food, seemingly endless parties, tourists, and tourists' money. Street vendors were stocking their wares, knowing that the celebration would bring foreigners with bulging pockets, more than willing to shell out a pretty penny for a trinket or two, a little something to remind them of their time in Rio. Women were preparing themselves for the foreign men— some familiar, others not so familiar—who would knock on their doors, aching for an exotic liaison that they could tuck away, deep in their memories and take back home with them when they returned to the wives they no longer desired and the children they'd grown tired of supporting. Other women and girls were scattered throughout the city, practicing dance steps and mouthing the words to songs as they prepared to wow the parade judges, their costumes hanging in their bedrooms, their hard work finally on the cusp of coming to fruition. But for Victor Castro, there was no anticipation, nothing to prepare for. The only thing he was sure of was the couch in his cousin's crowded apartment that served as his bed and his job washing dishes at the hotel where his cousin worked as one of the managers, both of which he abhorred, but when he left São Paulo and his mother and siblings behind, he'd vowed to himself that he wouldn't return until he had succeeded at something.

He wanted to drive home in a nice car, wearing nice clothes, with enough money to share with his mother who'd spent most of her life working hard to support her children. He wanted to be able to tell her he'd made the right decision in moving to Rio. The problem was that beyond regular schooling and his education at the English school, he had not received any training. There was nothing for him to be successful at. So he'd taken the job at the hotel with hopes of being able to move up to being a waiter in the hotel's restaurant pretty quickly. It had been six months and a promotion was nowhere in sight. As he lay on the sofa, listening to his cousin and her boyfriend argue, he closed his eyes and hoped he would soon be able to save enough money to get a place of his own.

***

Every morning, Victor rose with the sun, showered, dressed, and quietly left for work two hours early to avoid a confrontation with his Cousin Talita's boyfriend. He'd employed this method of keeping peace for two months and it had worked since Dimas was usually a late riser. And why not? He had no job, nothing to do but watch TV, eat, and drink beer all day. He'd told Talita on more than one occasion that he was tired of Victor being there. Victor never understood why or what he'd done to earn this man's ire, unless it was his looks. Victor was tall and beautiful with brooding amber eyes, thick curly hair, and deeply sun-kissed skin. Men tended to see Victor as a threat because of his looks. It had been that way since school. Even as a child, other boys disliked him because the teachers would dote on him. As a teenager, the girls would swoon over him. The only place he did not stand out was at home among his siblings who were all equally as striking.

Victor nodded and smiled at a street artist seated on a wooden crate stacking his canvases, paint, and brushes. He smiled at a shopkeeper unlocking his doors in anticipation of the day's customers. He nodded his head at an older woman who, along with her daughter, was preparing to sell *espetinhos* and *quiejo coalho*. Victor's stomach growled. In his haste to leave, he hadn't eaten breakfast. He'd try to sneak a snack once he made it to work.

Thirty minutes later, he'd arrived at his destination, a high-end hotel already bustling with activity and filled nearly to capacity with eager tourists. He quickly donned his kitchen uniform and went to work washing dishes.

2

"Rede de Espera" (Waiting Web)

Time always seemed to fly when Victor was at work. This was both a good and a bad thing. Good, because by the end of his shift he was exhausted and relieved for it to be over. Bad, because it meant he would have to return to his temporary home and listen to Dimas go on another drunken rant. Dimas never hit Talita, thank goodness, but Victor was always prepared to defend her if he did and was therefore always on the alert, listening for sounds of abuse. It was hard to relax, let alone sleep, under those conditions. What was worse was that Talita acted as if it was normal, as if being berated and called names was a standard occurrence. When Victor had offered to leave, believing he was the cause of their problems, Talita said, "No, stay. If you leave, he'll just find something else to be mad about."

Victor often wanted to ask her why she didn't just leave him or make him leave, but he knew that look in her eye—the same look his mother had worn as she watched his father brutalize either him or one of his siblings, but mostly him. His father seemed to have held a special vendetta against Victor and saved his worst savagery for him. Her look, his mother's look, was a look laced with both fear and utter devotion.

Victor shook the thoughts of the past from his mind as he finished the last of his work. He had just turned to leave when those working with him began moving at a frantic pace, whispering to each other as they lined up at the front of the crowded kitchen. The chef turned and looked at him, nodded for him to join them.

As Victor stood in line with the others, confusion spread across his face. What was going on? A second later, the door that led from the kitchen to the dining area flew open and in walked the hotel's general manager, followed by a white woman wearing a navy blue gown and long, white gloves. She was pretty in a plastic surgery kind of way. Her tanned, taut skin and obviously-bleached blond hair alluded to the fact that she was much older than she wanted to appear. Her face was stoic as her eyes roamed the kitchen staff. That is, until she fixed them on Victor. When her gaze met his, her eyebrows lifted ever so slightly and then she let her eyes glide over his entire person.

His facial hair belied his age, made him appear older, but she could tell he was much younger than her... and she liked that.

She shifted her focus to the chef and offered him her hand. Before she could speak, the hotel's manager said, "This is Mrs. Jennings. She wanted to pay compliments for her meal."

Mrs. Jennings smiled as she firmly gripped the older man's hand. "Yes, it was absolutely divine, Chef. The best meal I've had in ages. And the service was impeccable." She released his hand and turned to the manager. "I do have a question for you, though."

He nodded vigorously. "Yes?"

She slowly sauntered over to where Victor stood, her eyes trained on him. "Why is this young man not on the wait staff?"

"Uh-um..." he stuttered, turning to face the chef who shrugged in response. "I'm not sure. He is new here."

She tilted her perfectly made-up face to the side and said, "He would make a good addition. He would certainly brighten things up out there." She reached for his hand. "What is your name, young man?"

Victor understood English well, but the sudden attention had taken him aback, so he stared at the woman's outstretched hand and remained mute.

"Falar!" the manager said gruffly, which translates to "speak" in English.

"Does he not speak English?" Mrs. Jennings said in horror, as if she weren't in Brazil and the national language was not Portuguese.

"Yes, I do," Victor said softly. "My name is Victor."

5

She smiled, raised her hand a little to remind him that it was there. He took her hand in his and squeezed gently.

Mrs. Jennings pulled away, her eyes glued to the young man. "Victor, how nice. Hmm, I'd like for him to serve me in my suite tonight, that is, if he is available. I'm willing to compensate him myself. Would you like that, Victor?"

Victor was tired and though he hated going home to Dimas, he wanted nothing more than to collapse onto that couch and fall asleep. But he couldn't pretend the idea of making some extra money didn't appeal to him. So he said, "Yes," without looking to the manager for approval.

"Wonderful. I'm in suite 1321. I'll see you in say, an hour or so?"

Victor nodded as he nervously rubbed his hand through his hair. "Sim—*yes*."

***

Myra Jennings sat on the small sofa in her suite, her heart racing in anticipation of the arrival of what she hoped would be her next boy toy. At first sight, her body had reacted favorably to the bronze young man her eyes had graced in the kitchen. Young, tall, broad shoulders, nice arms, gorgeous eyes, pouty, kissable lips, and just the right amount of innocence.

Teachable.

She smiled as she brought the glass of vodka to her botoxed lips and sipped. She adjusted the belt on her silk robe and glanced at the clock. *I do hope this young man will be punctual*, she thought. There was nothing she hated more than tardiness, but she had a feeling this young man might be worth overlooking a little social ineptness or lack of decorum. Her body was on the verge of overheating just thinking about him and his huge, smooth hands. She couldn't wait to feel them against her silken skin.

She sighed as she glanced across the room at the photo that sat on the night table. She always took Bernard with her wherever she went.

He had been a good husband to her, even better after his death, having left the bulk of his estate to her after she persuaded him that his adult children, the products of his previous union, did not have his best interest at heart. Thanks to her inheritance, she spent every season in a different location—summers in Jamaica where her boy toy of choice was a striking, tall, dread-locked specimen by the name of Jorell. Oh, how Jorell could make her see heaven on earth. He was by far her favorite and the most adept of her temporary companions. She loved spending the summer months in a smeared-lipsticked, marijuana-induced haze—drinking rum, eating jerk chicken, and spending countless hours in bed inside of her late husband's island bungalow. She spent the autumn months on the French Riviera where Jean-Paul made her body sing with pleasure. Spring was spent in Italy with Giuseppe, who was her first lover when she was still married, before Bernard's death. Giuseppe was older than her other companions, but he was a master at romance, making her feel like there was no other woman in his life besides her when she knew better.

Winter was reserved for Brazil, for Carnival, and up until this trip, for Bolade, an Afro-Brazilian who, on a good night, could make her toes curl and her mind numb, and that was just what she needed—mind-numbing sex. She needed to forget that she was a lonely old woman whose wealth had only served to isolate her. She needed to forget the lies she'd told, the men of old she'd slept with as she made her way to Bernard's bed. She needed to forget the children she was never able to conceive, the friends whose husbands she'd bedded, destroying their bonds. She just needed to forget. *Period.*

When the knock finally came at the door, she glanced at the clock and thought, *right on time.* She stood from the sofa and slowly sauntered to the door, opening it to find the young man still in his kitchen uniform, his eyes full of curiosity. Myra Jennings smiled and stepped out of the doorway to allow him entry into her room.

Victor walked inside and stood by the door as she closed and locked it behind them. "At your service," he said, just as the general manager had advised him to.

Myra walked over to the sofa and reclaimed her seat. "Good to hear." She patted the vacant cushion next to her. "Come. Sit."

Victor hesitantly sat beside her. "Um, thank you. I am a waiter, now."

She flashed him a smile as she rested her hand on his knee. "You are more than welcome."

Victor flinched a little, surprised by her touch. "Um… how can I serve you, Mrs. Jennings?"

"First, you can call me Myra."

"Yes, Mrs.—Myra. What can I do for you… Myra?"

She lifted her hand from his knee, stood from the sofa, and shrugged out of her thin, silk robe, allowing the fabric to pool at her feet. She stood before him, naked as the day she was born, wearing a mischievous smile on her face.

Victor's mouth fell open at the sight before him—augmented breasts and liposuctioned everything else. This old woman had nipped and tucked her body into that of a teenager. He quickly dropped his eyes and frowned slightly. "I don't… what are you doing, Mrs.—Myra?"

"What does it look like?"

"Um…"

"I want you to pleasure me. You do know how, don't you?"

Victor stared at her, unsure of what he should do, thinking to himself that if he did what she wanted, he'd probably lose his job. Finding another one would not be easy.

"You do like girls, right? Surely, you do."

Victor nodded. "Yes, but—"

She lifted her eyebrows. "Oh, I see. Just a moment." She rushed to the closet, dug in her designer bag, and hurried back to him, dumping several one hundred-denomination *reais* banknotes into his lap.

Victor stared open-mouthed at the money. It would take him months to earn as much working in the kitchen. As he raised his eyes to face the woman again, a small smile played at the corners of his lips.

"For you, *after* you've pleasured me." She walked over to the bed and lay on her side, facing him. "Come, now."

Victor placed the money on the cushion beside him and then stood and pulled his shirt over his head as he made his way to the bed.

3

"Rio After Dark"

In the stillness of the early morning, Victor lay next to Myra Jennings, his mind reeling from the day's rapid succession of events as he relished the softness of the mattress beneath his body. He couldn't believe his luck. He was spending the night in a luxury suite with a pile of money awaiting him when he was ready to leave. And all he'd had to do was sleep with Myra, something he would've been willing to do for free after seeing her tight, surgically-sculpted body. He turned his head to face her, remembering what had occurred and reoccurred just hours earlier—bodies tangled beneath expensive covers, sweat and natural scents mingling, heated flesh merging, morphing into one body, cries of ecstasy, sighs of relief. Myra was insatiable, but so was Victor, and as soon as he realized she'd shed her inhibitions—or rather, that she didn't possess any inhibitions at all—he'd shed his, showcasing what he'd learned behind school buildings and in pink bedrooms whose windows he'd climbed through in search of a little teenage fun. He showed her what Ana Julia Silva had taught him to do with his hands in the basement of the little church they both attended as kids and what he learned to do with his mouth with Cybele Duarte one Saturday in her neat little bedroom while her single mother was at work and what he learned about a woman's body during the time he later spent with Cybele's single mother.

He smiled at how surprised she'd seemed at his skill level. He was young, just twenty-one, but he definitely wasn't inexperienced nor was he immature in any way, especially when it came to sex.

And now she knew.

He rolled over and stared at the bedside clock, watching as the bright red numbers changed from minute to minute, wondering if he should call Talita and tell her where he was. He knew she'd be worried, but it was near daybreak now and calling at this hour would probably upset her more than not calling at all. It would be time for him to report to work in a couple of hours. Maybe he could catch her during his lunch break and explain his absence from her couch. But what was he supposed to say to her? He couldn't exactly tell her he'd spent the night with one of the hotel's guests, an American woman who'd paid him, and paid him well, to have sex with her over and over again. To be honest, it didn't even sound believable, and the last thing he needed was for Talita to call and tell his mother. But he knew she'd do just that. And when his mother finished crying and confessing and praying for her wayward son, who, as she put it the day he left São Paulo, had fallen into the devil's trap inside of the devil's den—Rio—she'd show up at Talita's apartment and drag him back to her house. He couldn't let that happen. He couldn't go back home to the memories and ghosts. And besides, he liked having sex, even illicit sex, and really didn't want to hear his mother voice her feelings about the ills of fornication or the wages of sin, or anything else along those lines.

He rolled onto his back and sighed, wished he had ten times what Myra had paid him so that he could truly be independent. He closed his eyes and seconds later, felt her stir beside him. She laid her hand on his chest, let her fingernails graze his skin, asked, "Are you awake?"

Victor smiled and turned to face her in the darkness. "I have work soon."

"Your work is here. I'll talk to the manager. He won't object."

Victor was silent, thinking to himself that she wouldn't be able to talk to the manager after she left.

"I'll pay you double per day what I paid you last night. Just stay here. Don't leave. "

Victor's breath stopped for a moment. Double? "What will I do when you leave? My job. They may say fine now. But after you leave, they may change."

She reached over and caressed his stubble-covered cheek. "I will be here for six weeks. After that, we'll just have to find someone else to take care of you."

Victor frowned. "What? What do you mean?"

Myra rolled over, turned on the bedside lamp, and grabbed a cigarette. Without bothering to cover her nakedness, she lit the cigarette, took a drag, allowed smoke to seep through her thin lips, and said, "Darling, you are far too talented to be working in a kitchen or as a waiter." She turned and smiled at him. "Too talented and too handsome."

Victor lifted himself up on an elbow. "Talented?" If she was referring to sex, he'd never thought of that as a talent.

"Mm-hmm… Victor, how old are you?"

"Twenty-one."

"Twenty-one? You could pass for older and that's good. But then again, if you lose the facial hair, you'll appeal to the Mary Kay Letourneau types."

"Who?"

"Never mind that. Just know that if you play your cards right, you could have a wonderful career ahead of you."

"Career?"

She laid the cigarette in an ashtray and gave him her full attention. "Darling, I know women, *very rich women*, who will pay you handsomely for your time and your body." She shuddered as she eyed him. "*Especially* your body."

Victor stood from the bed and leaned against the wall. "I do not understand. You mean sex? Women will pay me for sex?" He knew prostitution could be a very lucrative business for many women and some men. But for him? He just couldn't imagine.

Myra laughed lightly. "Of course they will. Didn't I? The women I know will pay you for sex and they'll pay you well. But first we'll need to get you some clothes and a nice little love nest. But darling, you have what it takes. You caught my attention in a kitchen. With the right tools, women will be falling at your feet—*rich* women."

Victor pondered what she was saying, thought about the possibility of him earning the type of money he had with Myra on a regular basis in exchange for merely having sex, wondered if it was really possible. *It couldn't be*, he thought. With skepticism shadowing his face, he lifted one corner of his mouth and shook his head. "You are crazy."

Myra eyed his unclothed body again, leaned over the side of the bed, and rose with her purse in her hand. She dumped the contents onto the bed, opened her wallet, and pulled all of her cash out. She held it toward him. "Take it. You earned this and more."

Victor leaned forward and grasped the money, but Myra held onto it. "This is just a drop in the bucket in comparison to what the women I know will pay you. I'm poor compared to some of them." She released the money and raked the contents of her purse off of the bed then crawled toward him and grinned. "Now, come here and do that little thing you did with your hands again."

Victor smiled, dropped the money on the bedside table, and joined her in the bed.

4

"Incident in Rio"

Victor left Myra that afternoon with a promise to return later in the evening. He wanted to at least let Talita know he was okay before she called and alerted his mother, and he needed to gather some of his personal belongings to take back to Myra's suite. She had promised to take him shopping, but like any man would, he preferred wearing his own underwear and his own condoms, among other things. He smiled at the thought of his bulging wallet as he ascended the narrow stairs to his cousin's apartment. At the rate things were going, he'd be able to afford his own place in no time, and one ten times better than the one he was entering.

He was surprised to see that the pot-bellied Dimas wasn't passed out in his easy chair—surprised and delighted. He grabbed his bag (which he never really unpacked) from the living room closet and called his cousin's name. No answer, but he was sure she was there. He'd looked for her at the hotel before he left and was informed that she'd called in sick. Where else would she be other than home? He walked the few steps to the only bedroom in the small apartment and knocked on the door. "Talita? Talita, are you in there?" he asked in Portuguese. "It's me, Victor."

The bedroom door flew open to reveal a badly disheveled Dimas. Victor frowned. "Where is Talita? She is sick, yeah?"

Dimas glanced back into the room. "She is fine, sleeping."

Victor peered into the room, saw Talita lying in bed underneath the covers. "Are you sure she is okay?"

"You think I am lying?!"

Victor moved back a little. "I was just... Would you tell her I'll be spending some time with a friend?" He lifted his bag.

Dimas's eyes lit up. "So the pretty boy is finally leaving. Good. I was tired of you being here." He slammed the bedroom door, leaving Victor standing there with an uneasy feeling.

Later that night, after Myra was fast asleep, Victor took the suite's telephone into the bathroom and dialed a number he hadn't dialed in months. He knew he was running the risk of scaring her by calling so late, but Myra hadn't given him much of a choice. Pouncing on him the moment he returned to her suite, she'd seemed determined to make him earn his money and then some. The nice little bundle of cash she'd given him in addition to the wad he was already carrying had been a nice surprise, but at the rate they were going, he was going to need to take a trip to see a chiropractor soon. His young back was beginning to ache.

He stretched, moaned softly, and grinned. *This still beats washing dishes and mopping that disgusting kitchen floor*, he thought. As long as the money kept flowing in, he could deal with a few aches and pains here and there. As he sat on the toilet, his mother's groggy voice filled his ear. "Alô?"

"Mãe... Mother, it is Victor."

"Que saudade! Victor!! My heart has missed you so! Is everything okay?"

"Yes, I am fine. I... I miss you. I wanted to hear your voice."

"Ah, Victor. You are good? You are healthy? Sleeping well?"

"Yes, I am fine. I… ah, have a new job. I will send you money soon."

"A new job? What kind of job?"

"I... assist the hotel guests. It pays well."

"Oh, good! The manager must like you to give you such an important job. I am proud of you. How is your Cousin Talita?"

"That is why I called. I think you should talk to Uncle Artur. I think Talita is in trouble."

"Trouble?! Is she hurt?"

"I am not sure. It is her boyfriend."

"Dimas?"

"Yes, I think he might have hurt her. Something is not right. I know this, but since he dislikes me, I did not want to push it with him. He will have to respect Uncle Artur as her father, though."

"Yes, I will call him as soon as we hang up."

He and his mother chatted for a few more minutes, their conversation covering everything from what she cooked for dinner that evening, to the status of his oldest brother's rocky second marriage. When he finally rejoined Myra in bed, she said, "You have a lot to learn, my dear boy."

He turned to face her back in the darkness. "About what?" he asked, thinking to himself that surely he'd proven his sexual prowess to her by now.

"About women."

He sighed quietly, more than a little irritated with his benefactor. "And what is it I need to learn about women?"

"You need to learn that women, especially women who are willing to pay you handsomely for your time, do not like it when you sneak into the bathroom to call *other* women."

Incensed, Victor reached over and turned the bedside lamp on, sat with his back resting against the headboard, and said, "I was talking to my mother."

Myra flipped over and pushed the covers to the foot of the bed. With her eyes glued to his, she said, "That's even worse! No woman wants to sleep with a mama's boy! We like them young but we want them weaned! A mama's boy is a complete and utter turn-off!"

"I am not a mama's boy!" Victor shouted. A vein pulsed in his temple as he hit his fist against the thick mattress.

"Now *that* I like. That… that *machismo* you just showed? *Big* turn on."

Victor frowned. "What? What is machismo?"

Myra slid closer to him, rested her hand on his firm thigh.

"Machismo is a man being a man and we women love it."

Victor moved her hand, no longer enamored by this new career of his.

"Oh, come now. There is much to learn, but I will make sure you learn it all. Now, come, darling. Time for you to earn your keep. Bring that machismo over here."

He didn't budge. If this was what it was going to be like, dealing with jealousy and demands, he would've rather stuck to working in the kitchen.

She slid her hand over his thigh, caressed his bronze skin, and peppered his chest with soft kisses. "I'm sorry," she whispered. "Let me make it up to you."

Victor looked down at her and sighed. He remembered what his life had been like just days earlier—sleeping on a sofa in a place where he was not really welcome or wanted, working in the hot kitchen cleaning the remnants of expensive meals from plates, his mouth watering at the sight of the scraps. No, he didn't want to go back to that after all. So he reached over, turned off the light, and dutifully went about the business of satisfying his new employer.

5

"Knee Deep In Rio"

"*Você* me faz sentir tão bom," Myra said as they enjoyed breakfast together in her suite.

Victor smiled and tried not to laugh at her attempted pronunciation of the phrase; her Portuguese was horrible. He took a bite of fruit, pointed his fork at her, and said, "You make me feel good, too, Myra." It wasn't a lie. Myra was skilled in the bedroom, *very* skilled, and the steady flow of cash she doled out would make any man feel good.

"I am going to hate to leave you, my darling! You have been wonderful!"

"You have another two weeks here, yes?"

"Yes," she said, taking a sip of her Bellini from a spotless champagne flute.

Eyeing her, Victor mused that she was the only person he'd ever seen who drank nearly twenty-four hours a day. Silence fell between them for a moment.

"You need a place to stay," Myra said out of the blue.

"I have a place to stay," he said. It was almost a lie, but she didn't know that.

"I'm sure you do. Somewhere in some favela village, probably," she replied, her tone laced with disdain.

Victor wanted to argue with her, to tell her she was wrong, but she wasn't far from being correct. His cousin's apartment wasn't exactly in the slums, but it definitely wasn't paradise. "I will get one," he said softly, pushing his plate away.

"No, *I'll* get you one." She drained the flute and clumsily set it on the table. "Today," she added. She flashed him a slightly inebriated smile and beckoned for him to move closer to her.

Victor sighed inwardly. He loved sex as much as the next man, but Myra was proving to have a ravenous sexual appetite and that was putting it mildly. And her little remark about his living situation had not exactly put him in a love-making mood. Nevertheless, he stood from his chair and scooted it close to hers. Then he sat down beside her and gave her his best smile. "Yes?"

She giggled lightly as she caressed his cheek. "You are a handsome one. Hmmm, I think we should do it right out there on the balcony. Don't you?"

He shrugged. "If you would like that."

Her eyes narrowed as she leaned in and planted a sloppy kiss on his neck. "I would."

Victor stood from his chair, his youthful body at the ready as he reached for the older woman's hand. He resolved that maybe he'd been a little too gentle with Myra, had held back some of his best tricks. He would wear her out this time so that he could get some rest afterwards.

***

Victor wasn't expecting this, not *this* at all. Not a luxury penthouse, furnished to perfection. Not an ocean view. Not the lease with his name on it, paid up for a year. None of this was what he expected. As he stood in the middle of the living room taking in the sleek white furniture and spotless tiled flooring, he was at a loss for words. He rubbed his hand over the expensive blazer he wore—another gift from Myra—and wondered to himself if he was dreaming. He wondered if this was a fantasy he'd concocted in his mind. Was he really back at the hotel, in the stifling heat of the kitchen scraping the remnants of overpriced cuisine from plates? He wondered if he was actually asleep on his cousin's sofa, dreaming of a life that was so far out of reach it could never be his. Was he daydreaming like he often did as a boy when he wanted to escape the reality of sharing a home with a father who loathed him? Myra's sultry voice soon reminded him that he was awake, though, and that this was reality, a new reality for him.

"You like?" she asked as she plopped down onto the sofa and crossed her bare legs, allowing her short skirt to ride up her thighs.

"Yes, very much. Thank you, Myra," he said as he took a seat next to her and placed his hand on the warm flesh of her thigh.

She shuddered at his touch, remembering what he'd done to her on the balcony earlier. Up until that point, he'd been holding out on her. Oh, he'd been good from the start, but that morning had been mind-blowing! "Darling," she drawled, "oh how I wish we could christen this place right now. But I'm a little sore."

Victor smiled. "Really? You are sore? Why?" He leaned in, gently kissed her neck, and smacked her thigh.

She winced and closed her blue eyes. "You know why."

Victor cupped the side of her face and kissed her deeply. "Do I know?" he asked, enjoying teasing her. This part of the job, he liked. Playing games was something he'd always loved.

"You know you do." She gasped as he caressed her thigh where he'd smacked it and pulled up her skirt. "Victor, I can't..."

He lifted his head and looked her in the eye. "Oh, I think you can. You can and you will. You will let me thank you for my new apartment, yes?"

She stared at him, nodded breathlessly, and gave in.

***

Victor's first night in his new home was a surreal experience. After they christened the place, Myra had been anxious to leave, having given Victor another wad of cash and the night off. Victor spent the better part of the evening turning faucets on and off in the kitchen and bathroom, surfing the channels on the huge TV, and raiding the fully-stocked refrigerator. He'd taken a long shower, relishing the beating of the water against his bare skin, and was now sitting on his sofa, naked.

He wished he had a phone, but Myra had promised one would be installed the next day. He'd just have to wait to call his mother to check on Talita. When he and Myra left the hotel earlier, she was nowhere to be found. As a matter of fact, he hadn't seen her since that day at the apartment some weeks earlier. As he sunk into the soft couch cushions, he wondered if he should tell his mother about the apartment. He would love for her to see it, but one look and she would know he was into something she would deem wrong. How else could a man his age, a boy as far as his mother was concerned, afford a place like this? He shook his head and thought to himself that this place would have to be a secret until he could think of a way to explain his sudden good fortune that wouldn't upset his mother. After all, even if it wasn't illegal in Brazil, prostitution was taboo, especially in his devoutly religious mother's eyes, and that was exactly what he was—a prostitute, a male prostitute, a *highly paid* male prostitute, a gigolo. He felt no guilt about taking Myra's money and knew he'd feel no guilt about taking any other woman's money. He was being paid to provide a service, to do something it seemed he was naturally very good at and enjoyed. Who would feel guilty about that? What could be better than a life full of good sex and good money? It was easy living at its finest.

He stood from the sofa and crossed the room to the huge window that overlooked the beach and ocean. He opened the curtains wide, allowing anyone who could see him by the TV's glow full view of his exquisite body. He didn't care who saw. He'd never been modest or ashamed of his body. He was proud of it and his face and the power that came with looking the way he looked, but until the day he met Myra, he had no idea just how far-reaching that power could be. He hadn't a clue that women were willing to pay for his company and sex, but now that he knew, he planned to use his power for as long as he could.

He stood there for a long while, watching a scarce amount of people stroll up and down the beach, and wished he wasn't alone. As he turned and retreated to his new bedroom, he almost wished Myra was there with him.

6

"Brazilian Soul"

Late the next morning, Victor was awakened by persistent knocking at his front door and it took him a full five minutes to realize where he was. He climbed out of bed without bothering to dress, figuring it was Myra. He was unsure of the exact time but surmised it was too early for the phone company to be arriving. On second thought, he grabbed the sheet from the bed and wrapped it around his waist—just in case.

He sauntered to the door, silently hoping it was Myra and if it was, he had wicked plans for her. He opened the door without checking the peephole and on the other side stood a towering, dark-skinned man with sun-streaked dreadlocks and a bleached white smile.

"Ah, Myra said you were a pretty one. The woman tells the truth," the man said in a thick accent Victor couldn't quite place. He almost couldn't understand him.

Victor frowned, beyond confused. "Myra? Where is she?" He unsuccessfully tried to look past the broad-shouldered man.

"Not here," the man replied, his grin widening.

"Who are you? Did she send you here?"

"A friend, and yes, she did."

Victor's frown deepened and then his eyes widened with recognition. Was this what she'd meant when she said she'd have to find someone else to take care of him after she left? Had she left Rio? Was he expected to sleep with this man? Victor squared his shoulders and fixed his eyes on the man who outweighed him and was taller by a few inches. "I am not gay," he said emphatically.

The man stood there for a moment and then burst into booming laughter. "Neither am I, bredda."

"Who are you?" Victor repeated.

"Jorell, a good friend of Myra's and a teacher of sorts. She told me you had much to learn, bredda."

Victor stared at him for a few seconds, a little of his confusion dissipating. "You... you are..."

Jorell smiled and leaned closer to Victor, lowering his voice. "I am Myra's boy toy, too, her *beach boy*. Have been for a long time."

Victor was speechless. Why would Myra send this man to his door without telling him first? And what exactly was he supposed to teach him?

"Let me in, bredda. *Mi nuh bite*." The man's umber eyes twinkled as he spoke in his native patois.

As Victor allowed the man entry into his new home, he reasoned that if he knew Myra, surely everything would be okay. Then he reminded himself that he barely knew her, himself. He began to question what he was doing. Should he be spending so much time with and accepting so much from a woman he didn't really know? Standing there watching this man inspect his new apartment, he wasn't sure if he was making the right decisions.

Jorell plopped down on the sofa. "She set you up good, bredda. Never known her to do anything quite like this for a man before. I mean, this is *really* nice. You must truly be special."

"Where are you from?" Victor asked as he continued to strain to understand the man's words. At least he finally understood "bredda" to be "brother."

"Jamaica, bredda. Myra flew me here last night."

Victor sat across from him and nodded. "You say you are a teacher? What are you here to teach me?"

Jorell reclined and rested his arms on the back of the couch with that ever-present smile on his face. "How to make love to a woman."

Victor leaned forward and scoffed. "What? I do not need any lessons in that. Ask Myra."

"Ah, bredda, you are speaking of sex. There's much more to making love to a woman than just sex."

"Okay? You are the teacher. Teach. What is it I am not doing to please Myra? Because her money—and this place," he said, waving his hands around, "tell me I am doing all of the right things."

Jorell placed his right ankle atop his left knee and chuckled. "Myra is easy to please. She likes sex and that's really all she requires. You didn't even have to work to get her, for goodness' sake. But other women will require more of an effort."

Victor was no more enlightened than the moment he opened the door. This man was talking in riddles and Victor regretted answering the door at all. He sighed and hung his head in frustration.

"For instance," Jorell continued, "there is a woman I service quite frequently. She is rather... *heavy*, and her husband puts her down. How would you handle a woman like this?"

"I would make her feel as beautiful as she probably is."

"No, you make her feel *sexy*, *desirable*, like she is the only woman for you and you would die without her sex. There is a difference, bredda. You have to make her believe you crave her, can't get enough of her, and dream about touching her when she is not with you."

"I am to make her think I love her?"

Jorell shook his head. "No, bredda. Rule number one: never tell them you love them. They'll leave their rich husbands to be with you and expect you to take care of them if you do that. And whish! There goes your paycheck. Funds gaan!"

Victor straightened his posture, gave Jorell a confused look.

"It's about lust, bredda. *Lust*, not love. Ya bang their brains out, make them want you. Play the game. Don't tell them you love them, and most of all, don't fall in love with them. Lust makes money, not love. Love will send you to the poor house! "

"That will be easy. I could never love a woman like Myra. They think they can buy anything with their money."

"And they can, bredda. She bought you, didn't she?" He was grinning again.

"She bought my time," Victor countered.

"Same thing, bredda."

"No one owns me."

"Okay, how hard did she have to beg you to take her money?"

Victor was silent.

"See, women like Myra know what to look for—handsome, young, and poor. You want them to respect you, you gotta make them think you need their bodies, not their money."

"Okay, I am listening."

7

"Bom Conselho" (Good Advice)

Jorell left late that night after having told Victor all he could about the art of seduction—how to woo a woman, how to make her want you more than you want her, how to make her believe you desire her more than anything even when you want nothing to do with her, and how to cater to the most ridiculous whims and wishes. He told him of one of his clients who required him to dress as a postman and referred to sex as "delivering the mail." Jorell said he happily obliged because the woman was willing to pay a pretty penny for his cooperation. Then there was the client who preferred being intimate in public restrooms. He told him if there was anything he was unwilling to do, he should let them know up front, clear the air. Victor understood he should make his rates known to them up front as well, but in a discreet way.

He also told him he'd need a job, a real job. Something that gave him easy access to women. Jorell was a bartender at a popular tourist spot in Jamaica. This was where he met most of his clients, but he said women also approached him on the beach. The key, he said, was to be noticeable, but not appear to want to be noticed. He said Victor's looks had already given him that gift. The evidence was in Myra seeking him out the first time she saw him, but, as he said, Myra was looking for someone, *something*.

"Some women are here just to relax and get away from it all, not for sex like Myra," Jorell said. "You have to make *those* women want you. Those are the true goldmines."

"Why?" Victor asked.

"Because they will be caught off guard. You will be something extra for them, something they had not even thought about finding. And they will be so delighted they'll gladly empty their pockets for you… over and over again."

"Will women like Myra not do the same thing?" Victor asked. From where he sat, women like Myra seemed to have very loose and deep pockets.

"Yes, they will, but since they are looking for someone like you, they can easily find someone else like you. You are nothing more than an object to them and they will not hesitate to replace you. Why do you think she sought you out?"

"What do you mean?"

"She needed a replacement. Her regular 'Brazilian boy' was unavailable. Still is."

"Who was he?"

Jorell's brow furrowed slightly. "Why do you care?"

Victor wasn't sure why he'd asked that question, himself. He thought for a second and shrugged. "Maybe I want to thank him for my good fortune."

A smile spread across Jorell's face. "All I know about him is that his name is Bolade and she adored him… almost as much as she adores me." He checked his watch. "Ah, I must go. Myra is expecting me. We have lots of catching up to do." He stood and gave Victor a wink. "You should think of maybe being a hairdresser, something with your hands. You have nice hands."

Victor was a little taken aback by that last statement. He locked the door behind Jorell and thought to himself there was no way he would become a hairdresser. He'd have to think of something else. He held his hands in front of his face and appraised the smooth skin and long fingers and had to agree that they were indeed nice.

8

"Real in Rio"

Victor climbed out of his new car—another gift from Myra—and strode up the sidewalk toward his cousin's apartment. He wasn't sure why he was there other than the fact that he hadn't talked to her in weeks and he was sure she was worried about him. No one knew about his new place, not even his mother, and besides, he hadn't talked to his mother since that night in Myra's suite. He was almost certain his entire family was worried about him by now. Maybe Talita could relay the message that he was okay.

Before stepping onto the first step, he bent over and swiped dust from his Italian leather shoes. He raked his hands through his hair and took a deep breath before finally ascending the stairs. He still wasn't sure how he'd explain the clothes, the shoes, the car—*everything*. Hopefully, something, some believable lie, would come to him.

He knocked, took a deep breath, and waited. No answer. He knocked again, tried the knob but the door was locked. He yelled through the door, asked if anyone was home in Portuguese, received no answer. Finally, he dug his key out of his trouser pocket and let himself in. The apartment was just as he'd last seen it. Beer cans lined the coffee table, evidence that Dimas's daily routine hadn't been altered. The place was quiet, a little too quiet for Victor's taste. Something didn't feel right.

He slogged his way through the small apartment to the bedroom and that was when he saw her lying there in the bed. He rushed to the bedside table, grabbed the phone, and called for help; then he sat on the bed and cradled his badly bruised cousin in his arms. He gently shook her. "Cousin! Cousin, are you all right?!"

She didn't answer and Victor feared he'd arrived too late to save her.

He closed his eyes and prayed as he'd seen his mother do so many times after the dust settled from one of his father's enraged temper tantrums. He prayed that his cousin, his *favorite* cousin who'd taken him in and treated him so kindly, would be okay. When he heard footsteps in the front of the apartment, he gently laid her limp body back on the bed and rushed to meet the emergency medical personnel and direct them to his cousin. He stopped in his tracks when he saw Dimas standing in the middle of the living room looking dazed. When Dimas looked up at him, a grin slowly progressed across his lips and as he opened his mouth to say something Victor was sure would be insulting, Victor pounced on him, punching the older man in the mouth and knocking him to the floor. Though Victor was laid back and non-violent in nature, his only desire at that moment was to physically destroy Dimas.

"What is going on?!" Dimas screamed as Victor grabbed him by the collar of his wrinkled polo-style shirt.

"You killed my cousin!" Victor shouted.

Dimas's eyes grew wide as his bottom lip began to inflate. "Killed? Killed?!"

Victor dragged him to the bedroom door. "Look!"

Dimas's eyes took in the lifeless frame of his lover and he did something Victor never expected to see the indelicate man do. He began to sob. "I... I did not mean to hurt her. I... she kept getting in my face, fussing about the bills and me getting a job and I... I..."

Victor heard voices coming from the living room and against his better judgment, released a sobbing Dimas and left to see who else was there. This time it was the heavily-geared medical personnel. He directed them to the room, past Dimas who was seated in the small hallway holding his head. Victor was relieved when the men informed him that Talita was alive if only barely. When he turned to follow them out of the house as they wheeled the stretcher to the awaiting ambulance, he noticed Dimas had slipped out of the apartment.

***

After calling his mother and telling her about Talita, Victor sat in the hospital's waiting area and hoped and prayed his cousin would be all right. Talita was short and almost rail thin with long flowing black hair and an infectious smile. And she was kind to a fault. Most of their family had warned her not to take Victor in, fearing the handsome young man would be too wild for her to handle. What they failed to realize was how much Victor admired and adored his cousin. He would never disrespect her home. That was why he'd taken Dimas's taunts and abuse in silence. That was why he'd not intervened when Dimas and Talita argued. He respected her home and her desire to be in a relationship with the man, but Dimas had crossed the line and Victor was now determined to show him just how much of a man he was at twenty-one.

How could he hurt her like that? Victor wondered. *And why would she want to be with someone like him?*

Victor had actually asked Talita the very same question once and she'd said, "It's probably hard for you to believe this, but Dimas was very attractive when I first met him. He had muscles and women loved him. He had a good job and he spoiled me. Then he started drinking and everything began to fall apart."

Victor sighed as he leaned back in his seat and closed his eyes. What felt like ages later, he heard a familiar voice saying, "Victor? How is Talita?"

He opened his eyes to see his mother and uncle standing before him.

9

"Recado" (Message)

As Victor led his mother into his new home, he felt a sense of impending doom but he wasn't sure exactly why. His uncle had refused to leave his ailing daughter's bedside, so he knew she'd be safe from Dimas if for some reason he decided to visit her, therefore he had no need to worry about her. And his mother seemed to believe his story about his new job at the hotel. She didn't even seem surprised when they pulled up to the lavish apartment building that was his new home. She'd only nodded when he claimed the apartment and fancy car came with the job. He hadn't bothered to explain his clothes.

He supposed it was the idea of lying to his mother that wasn't setting well with him. He loved her, had forgiven her for failing to protect him from a monster of a father, and had grown closer to her as he transitioned into adulthood. He hated lying to her. He hated lying, period, because one lie always led to another, and soon the liar could, and probably would, lose track of all of the lies told.

Daisy Castro stepped into the plush apartment and raised her eyebrows. "You bought this furniture, Victor?"

He cleared his throat and gave her a nervous smile. "Yes," he lied... again.

She merely nodded as her chocolate eyes took in her surroundings. She stepped into the kitchen, her favorite place in any house, and ran her hands over the sleek counter tops. She opened the refrigerator and her eyes grew even wider at the array of expensive food that crowded the box. Victor watched her intently, silently chiding himself for not just getting her a room at a hotel. Why had he brought her *here?*

She smiled as she walked over to him and rested a hand on his cheek. "You have done so well! I am proud of you." She wrapped her arms around her boy and squeezed. Victor breathed a heavy sigh of relief.

"Dahhhhhling! Where have you been?! I have been waiting all day. I'm so hot for you. I'm on fire! *Quente!* I need you to come put me out!"

The voice came from behind Victor and it made his entire body stiffen, but he held onto his mother whose view of the woman was obstructed by her much taller son. Daisy looked up at her son with a frown and an obvious question in her eyes. *Who was that?*

Victor spun around, tried to keep his mother behind him, and instantly wanted to disappear. There stood his benefactor—nude, holding a half-empty glass of wine. "It's been *days*, darling. *Days*. I need you *now*. I want you to do that thing you do with your tongue."

"Um-uh-um, Myra, um-uh—"

"You look absolutely delicious in that suit! You should always wear suits… or nothing at all." She giggled lightly.

His mother stepped from behind him and shrieked at the sight of the naked woman. Victor grasped his mother's arm and ushered her to his bedroom. "Wait here," he said.

"Victor, who is that woman and why is she naked?!"

"Mother… just wait here."

"Victor!"

"Mother, I will explain. Let me talk to her."

When he returned to the living room, Myra was still standing in the middle of the floor, in the buff, with a look of irritation on her face. "What the hell is going on?! Who is that woman?!"

Victor frowned. "What are you doing here?" he hissed.

With raised eyebrows, she said, "Excuse me? Am I hearing you correctly? Did you just ask me what I am doing in the apartment *I* paid for?"

Victor glanced toward his bedroom and then back at Myra. She was speaking too loudly and he needed to figure out what he was going to do. He needed to get her out of there. His mind shifted quickly and he leaned in and kissed her deeply. He could feel her anger and tension disintegrate as she pressed her bare body against him. When their lips parted, he said, "I am sorry. You surprised me. I thought you were spending time with Jorell."

She smiled as she smacked her lips. "I sent him back home. Jamaica is for Jorell. Rio is for Victor."

"Did you sleep with him while he was here?" he asked, feigning jealousy.

"We didn't do much sleeping, darling."

Victor reached around and pinched her butt. "I am going to have to punish you for that."

She leaned in close and said, "I hope so, because I've been a very bad girl." She sighed. "Will you grab my fur from the coat closet? I'm going to leave you and your little friend. I suppose I should be proud of you for being proactive about finding clients. She's a hefty one, though. I didn't think you'd like that type of woman."

Victor frowned. "Client? Oh... yes. Yes, I love all women, especially curvy women." He retrieved her coat and handed it to her. "Where are your clothes?"

As she shrugged into the expensive coat, she gave him a sly smile. "*This* is my clothes," she said as she rubbed her hand over the fur. "Be at my suite first thing in the morning. No more new clients until after I leave, understand?"

He nodded. "Yes."

He shut the door behind her, closed his eyes, and leaned his head against the door. He'd only been standing there for a minute or so when he felt something hit his back. He spun around to see his mother's purse on the floor by his feet and his dear mother standing behind him, seething.

"Did you just throw that at me?" he asked.

"Sim!"

He bent over and picked it up. "Mãe... why?"

She stepped closer to him. "Because I did not raise you to be a whore!"

"I am not—"

"Do not lie to me! I heard that woman! She paid for this place and she wanted to have sex with you!"

"Mother... a lot of people want to have sex with me. That does not make me a whore."

"Tell the truth!"

"The truth?" He shook his head, crossed the room, and fell onto the sofa. "The truth is you are right."

She gasped and then began praying in Portuguese. She wailed, made crosses in the air, fell to her knees in the middle of the floor. If there had been sackcloth and ashes at her disposal, he was sure she would have gone full-on Old Testament on him.

"Mother, please stop. Please, get up," he said. He was tired, sleepy, exhausted from the day's events and his mother's dramatic reaction was just adding to his weariness. He shook his head and sighed.

"Why? Why, Victor? *Why?*"

He leaned forward and hung his head. "Why what, mother?"

"Why would you do this, live a life of sin like this?"

"I guess I am like my father," he said. "Only instead of hiring whores, I *am* one."

"Victor! How dare you speak ill of the dead!"

"Is it not true?"

She struggled to her feet and stood in front of her son. "What your father did and who he was is no excuse for what you are doing. Taking money from women? Fornicating? It is all sin."

"Then Mother, I have been sinning for a long time. I have been fornicating since I was a boy."

"You are still a boy."

"No, Mother. I am far from a boy. The woman who just left can tell you that."

Her open palm scorched his cheek. "You remember who you are speaking to!"

He frowned as he held the side of his face. She had never struck him before. That had always been his father's job. He looked up at her with a mixture of anger, fear, confusion, and disappointment on his face. He couldn't speak, couldn't find the right words to react to what she'd done. Her expression changed and as he stood from the sofa and silently began walking to his bedroom, she apologized profusely. Victor merely entered his room, closed the door behind him, and fell onto his bed.

***

Victor awakened to the familiar aroma of pão de queijo, a breakfast staple from his childhood. He rubbed his eyes and sighed, not quite ready to face his mother after last night's confrontation regardless of the goodness he knew she was preparing for him in his kitchen. He sat on the side of the bed thinking of Talita and Dimas, and then his mind quickly snapped to visions of a naked Myra. He couldn't lie and say he hadn't wanted to take her right there in the living room. Had his mother not been there, he surely would have done just that.

His mother.

Another sigh.

He rose from the bed, threw on a t-shirt to go along with his pajama bottoms, and left the safety of his bedroom to find her at his stove working up a sweat. He adjusted the air conditioning before taking a seat at the kitchen table. "Bom dia," he said softly.

His mother turned to face him and gave him a small smile. "Bom dia."

He stood and moved to the sofa. His mother walked into the living area, placed a plate of the aromatic cheese breads on the coffee table, and then leaned over and kissed his forehead. "Obrigado," he said.

She gave him a warm smile. "You are always welcome."

He didn't know what to think. He was sure she was still upset about Myra and his association with her. He didn't understand the change in her mood.

"Did you sleep well?" she asked as she took a seat next to him on the sofa.

"Yes. You?"

"Yes, this sofa is quite comfortable."

He dipped his head. "I meant for you to sleep in my bed. I would have taken the sofa."

She straightened her posture. "No, thank you. I would have worried about what you have done in that bed."

He thought about what he and Myra did on the sofa his first night there and the corners of his mouth curved into a grin.

"Victor... I know you are upset with me, but I only want the best for you."

"Look around, Mother. Is this not the best?"

"Yes, it is nice... all of it. But at what price? You are so young. Are you planning to spend the rest of your life being a slave to women like your *friend* from last night?"

He frowned. "I am no one's slave."

"You think you are not, but you are."

He leaned back on the sofa and rubbed his forehead. This was not how he wanted to spend the morning. He almost wished he'd followed Myra back to the hotel and spent the night with her. It would've been much more fun to wake up to her gratitude rather than his mother's scolding. "You would rather I wash dishes for the rest of my life?"

"No! You did not give it enough time. You could move up, become manager like Talita. You could have a future. There is no future in being a whore!"

"Do you see where Talita lives, *how* she lives? Look what I have! I would never have this if I had her job!"

"Victor, There is a way which seemeth right unto a man, but the end thereof are the ways of death!"

Victor sighed. "Please do not shout the Bible at me, Mother."

She stood and began to pace the floor. "Does it not bother you to sin like this day after day? I did not teach you to live like this."

He looked at his mother and shook his head. "I just want to have something, to *be* something. This sin is the only thing I am good at. It is all I have right now and when I grow tired of it, I will stop."

She paused and stared at him. With sadness in her eyes, she said, "With sin, my son, you must reach the pit before you grow tired of it, and by that time, you will have nothing good left."

"I grew up in the pit, remember? And until now, I already had nothing."

She sighed softly and continued to try to reason with him. "You will probably never marry or give me grandchildren. You will always be *this* even when you are not *this*."

"Will you love me any less for being *this*?"

"No, but you must know you are breaking my heart… you are breaking my heart, Victor."

He dropped his eyes. "I am sorry for that, but being poor and having nothing was breaking *my* heart. I am a whore. Your fussing will never change that."

"Maybe my prayers will… one day."

***

After he dropped his mother off at the hospital to check on Talita who was improving, he drove straight to the hotel and rode the elevator to Myra's floor. He knocked on her door, watched as she opened it wearing nothing but a thin robe and a slight smile, anticipation in her eyes. He stood there for a moment, staring at her, trying to clear his mind of his mother's words, but *slave* and *whore* and *sin* kept bouncing around in his head like a brand new, perfectly-inflated basketball. He stepped inside, grasped her thin arm, and forcefully pulled his generous patron to him, pressed a hard kiss to her eager lips, and ripped her robe as he undressed her in seconds.

"The door is still open," she said as he began to disrobe.

He gave her a wicked smile. "I know."

He took her to her bed and spent the next two hours taking his frustrations out on her with the door to her suite ajar.

***

Myra stared at the open door, wondered how many people had heard her screams of pleasure, seen her limbs entwined with Victor's, felt the earth beneath them shake when they reached the pinnacle repeatedly. She placed a cigarette between her lips and inhaled. "You're going to get me kicked out, darling. This is my favorite hotel."

Victor glanced at her and then sat up in the bed. "Do you want me to stop pleasing you?"

"Hmmm, please don't."

"Then be quiet. If I want the door open, it stays open."

She grinned widely. "Yes, sir."

He ducked his head under the covers and she closed her eyes in anticipation of more pleasure—Victor-style.

10

"Rendezvous In Rio"

Victor was exhausted from spending more than a week chauffeuring his mother and uncle to and from the hospital to check on Talita and stealing time to spend with the rapacious Myra Jennings. The day Talita was discharged, he'd had to quickly take his relatives to her apartment, help her settle in, and then rush to the hotel to see Myra off. She was leaving Rio. A part of him would miss her. More than a part of him would miss her money. But a greater part of him looked forward to finding new clients, making new connections and even more money. He had settled in his mind that this was the career for him. His mother was still not pleased and he'd often caught her praying over him when she thought he was asleep at night. He understood her worry, but this was the only chance he had to be a success. He was good at pleasing women, *damn good*, and he was determined to take advantage of his newfound good fortune while he could.

On the ride to the airport, he tried to pay attention to what Myra was saying but he couldn't. There was too much on his mind. His cousin still was not safe. Dimas was not at the house when he dropped his family off, but the thought never left his mind that he could show up at any moment. His uncle wouldn't be able to protect both his mother and Talita from him at the same time. As the limo drew nearer to the airport, Victor's entire being began to fill with dread. What if Dimas was at the apartment right that second? What if he hurt Victor's mother?

"Darling, you haven't heard a word I said. What's in that pretty head of yours?"

He looked at her and didn't want to sound weak, but she was leaving anyway, and everything in him told him he needed to get back to Talita's apartment *now*. "My cousin is in trouble. I... I need to check on her." He glanced out the window. "Have the driver stop here. I will find a way to her."

She frowned. "Nonsense! I will not have my pretty boy out walking the streets like a vagrant. Tell the driver where you need to go."

"You will miss your flight."

"Darling, I'm rich. I can buy another ticket. Don't you worry about me. Let the driver know where to go."

Victor leaned in and gave her a passionate kiss before knocking on the partition.

Myra smiled as she gently rubbed a finger across her plump lips. "Hmm, was that a promise?"

Victor flashed her a smile as he turned to give the driver directions to Talita's apartment.

***

Once they arrived in front of Victor's old home, he turned to Myra and said, "Stay here. I just need to check on her. I will be quick."

She placed her hand on his stubbly cheek. "Take your time."

Victor stepped out of the limo in his expensive slacks and open-collared Oxford shirt and quickly made his way to the building. He bounded up the steps and was at his cousin's door in no time, using his key to let himself in. He was greeted by shouts and terrified screams coming from the bedroom. He rushed to see what was going on, stopped in the doorway to the room, and tried to take in the scene. Talita and his mother were huddled in a far corner, both crying loudly. There was blood on the sheets of the bed. And at the foot of the bed were his uncle and Dimas, locked in battle. From his vantage point, it wasn't hard to see who had the upper hand, and knowing that his uncle had several years on the much younger and larger Dimas, he knew he needed to intervene.

He entered the room and slapped Dimas on the back of the head, causing him to loosen his grip on Victor's uncle. Dimas spun around with a look of surprise on his face. "You!" he shouted.

"Yes, me!" Victor replied. Then he punched Dimas in the nose.

"Victor!" his mother shouted.

He ignored her and hit Dimas again. His uncle breathlessly cheered him on, glad to be relieved of his fighting duties.

Dimas threw a punch that barely grazed Victor's jaw and shouted, "I hate you, pretty boy! I always have!"

"Good, because I hate you, too!" Victor said as he lunged for Dimas, knocking him to the floor. He straddled the bigger man, pummeling him in the face too many times to count as his family members' voices filled his head—his mother begging him to stop and his uncle egging him on, all while his cousin wailed helplessly. He couldn't obey his mother and he didn't need his uncle's encouragement. His anger over Dimas's treatment of his dear cousin was all the fuel he needed to continue. If he had his way, he would make Dimas disappear.

"Victor! Bolade! What is going on?"

That voice, the voice of the munificent Myra Jennings, stopped him. He frowned as he looked up at her standing in the doorway draped in fur with a look of horror on her face. "Myra?" He looked down at Dimas whose face was covered in blood, his eyes fluttering as he threatened to lose consciousness. "Bolade?" Victor said softly.

"What is going on here?" Myra repeated. Her eyes drifted over the room. "Are you and Bolade fighting over your client?! I thought you needed to check on some cousin of yours! And Bolade, where in hell have you been? I went by our old place when I arrived in town and you were nowhere to be found."

Victor's mind raced. Client, what client? Then he remembered that Myra thought his mother was a client. But why was she saying these things to Dimas? She had to be mistaken. No way was Dimas ever a gigolo, not according to what Jorell had taught him. Gigolos were supposed to be smooth, charismatic, caring, accommodating, selfless, commanding, and irresistible all at the same time. Dimas was none of that. Victor couldn't see why any woman would pay to spend time with a brute like him. And besides that, he didn't possess the physique for this particular line of work.

Victor glanced down at his broken opponent again and then fixed his eyes on Myra. "Myra, I told you to wait," he said, giving her the machismo she craved.

She blushed and rubbed a gloved hand over her own cheek. "Yes, darling... I know, but I simply *have* to use the facilities and I saw you enter this apartment and—wait, I already asked *you* a question. Are you fighting over this woman?" She pointed at Victor's mother. "Are you and Bolade fighting over *her*?!"

"No—and his name is not Bolade, it's D—"

"And I am his mother, not his client, you Jezebel!" Daisy Castro launched into a spirited stream of Portuguese as she glared at Myra.

"Mother?! Victor, you said she was a client," Myra said through tight lips.

"I did not say that. You assumed so."

"Well, you didn't deny it."

Victor stood, stepped closer to Myra, and grasped her arm. "Let me show you out."

She snatched away. "No! I must know what is going on." She turned her attention once again to Dimas. "Bolade, where have you been?"

Dimas frowned and groaned, rolled over on his side and clutched his head.

"He cannot talk to you right now."

"Because you beat him up?"

Victor shrugged. "Yes."

"Why?"

"It is personal and does not involve you or any other client. I'll take you back to your limo, yeah?"

"I still need to use the facilities, and I want an explanation from

Bolade."

Victor sighed, turned to his uncle, and asked him to help Dimas onto the bed, then directed Myra to the small bathroom. He knew it wasn't going to be easy to get rid of her since she was convinced she knew Dimas, and he regretted taking her limo to the apartment.

While Myra relieved herself, Daisy helped Talita gather herself. Talita sat at the opposite end of the bed, eyeing Dimas, waiting for him to jump up and attack her again at any moment. Though she loved him and had tried everything in her power to make their relationship work, she now realized the true danger of trusting him. She had been the one who'd let him in. While her father and aunt congregated in her small kitchen, she'd answered the door and took him at his word when he said he was sorry for hurting her and just wanted to talk. No sooner than she opened the door wide enough for him to slide in, he'd attacked her, chasing her to her bedroom where her father had to peel him off of her.

She closed her eyes, remembering how kind he was to her when they first met. Kind and generous. She would never understand what made him change. After he moved in with her, he became a mean, unemployed drunk.

Myra emerged from the bathroom shaking her hands with a scowl on her face. "There was no hand towel. What kind of place is this?"

Daisy said, "*Cadela*," or, *slut*, in Portuguese.

"What was that?" Myra asked.

This time in English, Daisy said, "I called you a—"

"Myra, can we leave now?" Victor interrupted.

"No, I need answers from Bolade."

Victor released a frustrated groan. "This is Dimas, Dimas Cirino. He's my cousin's boyfriend. This is her home. This man is not *your* Bolade."

"No, this is *Bolade Varela*. He's gained weight, but I'd know him anywhere. I have known him for years and up until this year, he had *your* job. I paid his rent and I paid for his time and I came to Rio weeks ago to find that he was not where I left him. The apartment was empty." She leaned over until she was in Bolade's, or Dimas's, bloody face. "Where... were... you?"

Dimas looked up at her helplessly and with a slight lisp said, "The landlord found out about my... business, and since he was a preacher, he kicked me out shortly after you left last year. I couldn't reach you and I was already seeing Talita, so she let me move in with her. Because of having no other job and having to live here, I lost touch with my clients. And the few I was able to contact, I could not bring here and they wanted to meet somewhere other than their own hotel suites. Most of them came here with their husbands and depended on me to provide a place... and I couldn't." He shook his head. "And I hate it here. I hate being poor. I hate hearing her nag me about getting a job. I hate her pretty-boy cousin." He gave Myra a pleading look. "Take me with you, Myra."

Myra stared at him and then burst into raucous laughter. "Take you with me? Oh no, dear. You have been replaced..." She gave Victor a seductive smile. "With a better model. Isn't he just delectable?! He's so good, I got him an even better place than the one I got you... *much* better. I should thank you for disappearing, actually." She moved closer to Victor and softly kissed his cheek. "I'm heading out to the limo. Want me to wait for you?"

Victor smiled. "Yes, just give me a moment."

He escorted her to the door and then returned to the bedroom. His mother started to speak but he held up his hand to stop her. He pulled up the legs of his expensive slacks and squatted before Dimas. "I want you to leave here and never come back. If you do come back, if you ever touch my cousin or anyone else in my family again, I will kill you."

Dimas rubbed his jaw. "Myra replaced me, she will replace you, too."

Victor shrugged. "I do not care about Myra. She can replace me and I can replace her because I am very good at what I do. Some say I am the best. I *do* care about my family. That is all I care about. Go, and do not come back."

Dimas struggled to his feet and glanced at his lover. "I'll go. I do not care about her anyway. She is too skinny and her sex is bad."

Talita moved toward him with the help of Victor's mother and spat in his face. "*Bunda!*"

Dimas wiped his face with the palm of his hand. And then he left.

11

"Río-Líze"

"*Is* everything okay now?" Myra asked as Victor finally slid into the backseat of the limo.

"Yes. My mother and uncle are going to stay with my cousin. Dimas, uh, Bolade has left."

She knocked on the partition, giving the driver the go-ahead to leave. "Hmm," she said, "I wonder which is his real name?"

Victor shrugged. "I do not know, nor do I care."

"Well, I always knew there was something about him I didn't like. I never really trusted him."

"Why did you... hire him, then?"

"Well, he had the body of a Greek god when I met him and his skills in the bedroom were par excellent, that's why."

Victor nodded slightly and grew quiet, shifting his attention to the blurred scenery outside the tinted limousine window for several minutes.

"Oh, darling... did I hurt your feelings? Are you jealous?"

Victor turned to face her and shook his head. "Never," he said, then he leaned in and kissed her deeply. She panted as he began to strip her clothes off of her.

As the limo pulled to a stop in front of the airport terminal, Myra said, "Victor... my flight..."

"As you said, you are rich. You can buy another ticket."

***

Victor reclined on the sofa in his apartment, his mind full of the past few days' events as he relished the fact that Myra was now... somewhere. He wasn't sure where her next destination was, but he was glad to be able to meet new people, new clients, and make even more money. His mother and uncle had returned to São Paulo and his cousin was staying with him for a while, just to be safe. He was more than happy to provide her with a safe place to stay and return the kindness she'd shown him. However, his kindness had reached even further than hers as he'd given her his bed. He would sleep on the sofa.

He closed his eyes, recalling the last conversation he had with his mother before she left Rio. She'd said she was proud of how he defended his cousin, but that she despised Myra Jennings for pulling him into a life of sin. "I hope and pray you will one day choose another profession, one that will not send your soul to hell," she'd said.

Victor had rested his hands on her shoulders, locked eyes with her, and said, "I love you, Mother, and I appreciate any prayer you pray for me. But this is my life now and it just began. Maybe I will grow tired of it one day, but not today. I love you and I always will. I hope you will always love me despite my sins."

She'd reached up and rested her hand on his cheek. "Of course. Always. And I will pray that one of the women you... I will pray that one of them changes your heart and mind for the better. I pray that God sends someone to turn your whole world upside down."

He'd smiled at her and kissed her cheek before seeing her and his uncle off.

"Victor?" A soft voice interrupted his reverie. It was Talita standing over him. "Did I wake you?"

Victor shook his head as he smiled up at his cousin. "No, no, is there something you need? Sit."

She took a seat beside him and said, "I just want to thank you again... for everything."

"You are welcome. I owe you."

She smiled. "And now, *I* owe *you*. I will have to find a way to repay you."

He smiled and they sat in silence for a while. His first thought was to tell her no repayment was necessary, then another thought came to him. "There is something you can do for me... at the hotel."

She frowned slightly. "What is it?"

"I want a job. A better one. You will help me, yeah?"

She sat forward a bit and nodded. "Sure, sure, bellhop, front desk, whatever you want. I will make it happen."

"Masseur. I want to work in the massage parlor."

"Oh... I did not know you had trained as a masseur."

"I have not, but I learn quickly. I want to work with my hands."

"Okay, I will see what I can do. Aunt Daisy will be pleased to know you decided to get a different job. I am glad, too. I would not want you to end up like Dimas-uh-Bolade."

Victor grinned and thanked her.

12

"Depois do Carnaval" (After Carnival)

Six Months Later

Victor boarded the elevator and sighed. It was late and he was drained from a long day of working in the massage parlor, but his newest client awaited him and the money he anticipated earning instantly energized him. He eyed the leggy blond woman standing at the back of the elevator as he pressed the button on the panel. As the elevator began to ascend, he could feel her eyes on his back. He turned to face her. She smiled and licked her lips.

"Can I help you?" he asked.

She slowly moved towards him with a sly smile, slid a wad of money into his back pants pocket, and quickly gripped his butt for good measure. "I believe you can."

He took her into his arms and kissed her deeply while reaching for the button to stop the elevator. As he eased her skirt over her thighs then spun her around and pressed the side of her face against the elevator wall, she said, "I can't believe this is happening! I've always fantasized about being intimate with a stranger in an elevator."

She was trembling with excitement. She'd heard wonderful things about this young gigolo and was more than willing to pay to experience them herself, especially after the magical massage he'd given her earlier.

Victor moved her hair aside and whispered in her ear, "Shh, tonight I make all your fantasies come true, yes?"

Bonus Tracks:

"Splackavellie" *Pressha*

"Tease Me" *3T*

"Aim to Please" *Ife*

"Any Time, Any Place" *Janet Jackson*

"Lusty Lady" *Tom Jones*

For international domestic violence resources, visit:
http://www.vachss.com/help_text/domestic_violence_intl.html

If you or someone you know is a victim of domestic violence, visit:
http://www.thehotline.org/ or call **1-800-799-7233**

Learn more about help for victims of domestic abuse by visiting:
http://www.helpguide.org/articles/abuse/help-for-abused-and-battered-women.htm

For more information about Adrienne Thompson, visit:
http://adriennethompsonwrites.webs.com

Sign up for Adrienne's newsletter here:
http://eepurl.com/jnDmH

Follow Adrienne on Twitter!
https://twitter.com/A_H_Thompson

Like Adrienne on Facebook!
https://www.facebook.com/AdrienneThompsonWrites

Join Adrienne's Facebook group!!
https://www.facebook.com/groups/674088779363625/

Follow Adrienne on Pinterest!
http://www.pinterest.com/ahthompsn/

Connect with Adrienne on Goodreads!
https://www.goodreads.com/author/show/5051327.Adrienne_Thompson

Also by Adrienne Thompson

The *Bluesday* Series:

Bluesday

Lovely Blues

Blues In The Key Of B

Locked out of Heaven (Tomeka's Story – A Bluesday Continuation)

The *Been So Long* Series:

Rapture (A Been So Long Prequel)

If (Wasif's Story) A Been So Long Prequel

Been So Long

Little Sister (Cleo's Story—a companion novel to Been So Long)

Been So Long 2 (Body and Soul)

Been So Long III (Whatever It Takes)

SEPTEMBER (The Christina Dandridge Story—a Been So Long companion novel)

Been So Long IV (Rhythm of Love)

The *Your Love Is King* Series:

Your Love Is King

Better

The *Ain't Nobody* Series:

Sedução (Seduction)—an Ain't Nobody Prequel

Ain't Nobody

The Latter Rain Series:

After the Pain

No Pain, No Gain

Joy and Pain

The *See Me* Series

See Me

See Me, Too

Stand-alone novels:

Home

When You've Been Blessed (Feels Like Heaven)

Summertime (A Novella)

Fiction Anthology:

The Ex Chronicles — as a contributor

Nonfiction Titles:

Just Between Us (Inspiring Stories by Women) —as a contributor

Seven Days of Change (A Flash Devotional)

Poetry:

Poetry from the Soul… for the Soul, Volume II

All books are available at amazon.com, barnesandnoble.com, and kobobooks.com

Please enjoy this excerpt from *Ain't Nobody*
(Now available in Kindle, Nook, Kobo, and paperback):

Prologue

Sometimes a woman's just had enough. No matter how she may feel about a man. No matter how much she loves him and wants to be with him, there's always that one, teeny tiny little straw—the *last* straw. It usually pops up after she's done all she can humanly possibly do to make things work. She's cooked for him, cleaned for him, praised him, had sex with him, ignored his annoying ways, and yet, she still finds herself holding the short end of the stick.

As I sat there on the side of Quincy's bed, the last straw flew in through the bedroom window and landed right on my camel's back. Quincy, my fiancé and the love of my life, was in the shower whistling. He was whistling like he didn't have a care in the world. He was whistling like I wasn't thirty-seven and kicking the hell out of forty. He was whistling like I wasn't unmarried and childless. Like we hadn't been engaged for five years. *Five years*. He was whistling like he hadn't refused to set a wedding date. Like my biological clock wasn't ticking as loud as a time bomb.

I'd been with Quincy Wright for eight years. I'd been his lover and friend. I'd bent over backwards, neglected my own needs, and done all I could do to be a good woman. I wanted a husband and I wanted children and he knew it. We'd discussed it *at length*. And what was his response? His black behind was in the shower whistling. That was it, and whether he knew it or not, it was over. O-V-E-R.